About the Author

Michelle Raaf Chiusano is a teacher born and raised in Rockaway Beach, New York. She is married to her husband, Joe. She has a younger sister, Ashley, a mom, Laura, and a dad, Richard. She loves her hometown, family and of course her dog, Champ.

Champ's Day Out

Michelle Raaf Chiusano

Champ's Day Out

Nightingale Books

NIGHTINGALE PAPERBACK

A CIP catalogue record for this title is
available from the British Library.
ISBN 978-1-83875-396-2

Nightingale Books is an imprint of
Pegasus Elliot MacKenzie Publishers Ltd.
www.pegasuspublishers.com

First Published in 2021

Nightingale Books
Sheraton House Castle Park
Cambridge England

Printed & Bound in Great Britain

Dedication

This book is dedicated to my loving family,
thank you for always supporting me.

"Good morning, Champ, I missed you while you were sleeping!" I hear my mommy say. Champ, that's my name, time to get up and start the day!

I make sure to stretch and give Mommy a kiss,
telling her too, she was also missed.

We start to get ready, my collar goes on first. Mommy grabs a cup of coffee to quench her thirst.

She's finally ready to go after putting on her shoes. I'm so lucky I don't have any 'to do's'.

The elevator finally comes, we live high up. I love to sniff our neighbors, they always say, "What's up?"

We get to the lobby and stop to see ChaCha.
She is my best friend, besides my papa.

My nose sniffs out the beach, I love the smell of the salty air. I can't wait to go, we are almost there!

We first walk over to the park.
The kids are playing so I say
hello with a friendly bark.

Up next we pass the hockey rink where they play something funny. The humans roll around in such a hurry.

We see my buddy Ashley, she loves to skateboard here. She makes sure she is safe by wearing all her gear.

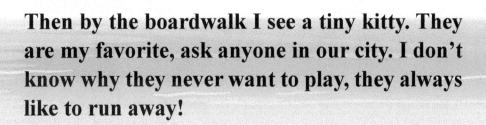

Then by the boardwalk I see a tiny kitty. They are my favorite, ask anyone in our city. I don't know why they never want to play, they always like to run away!

Mommy and I get to the beach. "Would you believe it," she cries, "a whale just breached!"

I get so excited but I'm not sure what to do so I take of toward the water, wouldn't you?

The sand is so wet, the ocean so cool. I go to put my paws in but before I do I look back at Mommy to get the okay.

She says, "Go ahead, Champ, go in and play."

I don't wait another second and go catch my first wave. Today I am feeling very brave.

"Champ, come look!" Mommy calls to me. I run over, get closer and what do I see? A shell, she found one and just the right type!

She throws it for me to fetch before I put up a fight.

I chase down the shell and dig a big hole. I'll just store it right here by this wooden beach pole.

Soon I get tired, I've played too much. Mommy says, "Champ, let's hurry up." I don't know why, but she's in a rush.

We get back home, I'm sleepy
now. We open the door and all
I want to do is lay down until
I hear a voice that I definitely
know. YAY it's my daddy, his
name is Joe.

My tail won't stop wagging,
I forget all about my shell.
I can't believe this was the
secret my mommy didn't tell.

We all go to sit down so I can get a belly rub. This was the best day ever I think, until I saw the bathtub!

CPSIA information can be obtained
at www.ICGtesting.com
Printed in the USA
BVHW020203281021
620169BV00016B/609